THIS IS FOR KEVIN JOSEY
WHO WANTED ME TO
WRITE SOMETHING FOR
THE GAY COMMUNITY
THAT MIGHT BE EROTIC
AND FUN AND SO HERE IT
IS!

BITCHES DON'T HATE!
LOVE YOU ALL!
DANA

"JOSEY K."

WRITTEN BY

ANAD (DANA) SENIH

HE WAS RUNNING LATE! He wanted to be the first in line at the Louis Vuitton store; he was told that person gets 75% off for being a valid customer.

Josey had called an Uber he was not risking getting his own speeding ticket he would just simply offer the driver

$20 bucks to haul some ass and get him there.

He would go to the Starbucks nearby for coffee so he was not wasting time brewing a fresh cup at home. He had to be there on time. SHIT! That's a $500 savings on the briefcase he wanted or more. For work he had to have the #1 look when he hit the door because #2 had too many applicants who fell through the cracks and ended up there.

The driver showed up in a nice Buick four door looking good and he was extremely handsome like one of those dark hairy muscular guys from Dubai. He had a huge chest that was accented well by heavy muscles like guns in his arms. He stood about six feet four when standing and Josey was already thinking of all the things he could do with his body, nasty things.

"Good Morning! Sir!" The driver spoke.

"Good Morning to you too now take this twenty dollars and see how much faster you can get me to my destination! I am on a mission! With your handsome self! Dam you looking good today!" Josey told him

"HA!HA! Thank you Sir! I am use to men complimenting me or offering to suck my dick or invite me in their home and women as well! I get my ample supply of pussy and ass from this job. I haven't jacked off in a year!" He told Josey.

"Hmm! Well save my number in your contacts I sure could use you on my back for a deep tissue massage soon! Maybe this afternoon?" Josey inquired.

"A guy like yourself can make me extra horny for long sessions for hours if you are submissive to me." He told Josey.

"Oh! You can bring your rope and handcuffs and take what you want with me. I am very curious and interested in leather community type sex. So just pound all you want! Yes Please!" Josey suggested.

"Do you like threesomes I have a well hung cousin that loves smaller guys like you we would tag fuck you for hours and he is very oral like me we lick you where its hot got to hit the spots!" He told Josey.

"What's your name you keep driving! If you fuck like you drive we going to have a good ole time in my sling!" Josey said.

"OMG! You have a SLING IN YOUR HOUSE? You are a GOOD FREAK! I will sit in a chair and eat your out after we load you with our cum! I love HOT SEX!" He told Josey. "My cousin will too!" He added.

"I am Rahoul my number is 776 554 3001 PLease text me now baby I want your pussy so bad!" Rahoul said.

Rahoul's phone received a text and an ass pic from Josey's phone. Rahoul begged him to reach up front and feel how big and hard he made him. Josey actually was frightened by the size of his dick it must be 12 inches and fat as a Coke can he was in for it.

"Do you like and want me? I am not small." He asked Josey.

"I am not afraid of dick I want you and your cousin too!" He answered.

They had arrived at the store and noone was lined up So Josey reached up front to snag a deep tongue fucking kiss from Rahoul who reached behind Josey to grab his ass and squueze his cock as well.

Rahoul jumped at the moment to open Josey's door so he see his massive hard on pointing down his pants and Josey squeezed it and almost kissed it he got so hot for he loved giving head to a big dick man.

Josey walked in a hurry to Starbucks to get his coffee and a muffin for breakfast. It ended up being free with so many points he had built up.

Then he was off to get that 75% discount even though Rahoul was all the discount he needed. Dam that dick is going to rip his ass good!

The door was unlocked and sure enough the sales staff applauded as he was given the 75% off coupon for today.

"YES BITCHES!" He said out loud. Then off to luggage he went hoping they have it in stock to take with him.

SURELY IT WAS IN BROWN AND GOLD!
He approached a blond handsome tall salesman with a black girl's ass, a

bubble of joy Josey would love to taste.

"DAM! You have any luggage that can fit in? Its fucking nice! You got me rock hard in this store!" Josey told him.

"NOW! NOW! Lets get your purchase done and get me on the books then we can play." The salesman told him. The salesman liked what he saw and he too had a raging hard on showing in grey slacks it was something fat to see in his slacks.

Wow! The early birds do get the worms! He laughed. As he adjusted his own hard cock he needed a wet throat.

Josey paid and the clerk sent the case up front so he can pick it up on the way out.

"Follow me!" he told Josey

They strolled towards the private key locked changing rooms and both entered as Josey sat on the settee the salesman pulled Josey's pants off and shoes and placed them on the seat.

He wasted no time sucking Josey's fat cock working the head with tongue and lips and swallow to the balls
Josey fucked his throat for about five good minutes both keeping their rhythm and Josey BUST RIGHT IN

HIS MOUTH! A FULL MORNING LOAD.

The salesman didn't spill a drop he swallowed and almost begging for more so Josey turned and offred his ass which the salesman devoured with a sloppy wet tongue. Josey now could see the huge cock he was jacking right before he pushed it balls deep in Josey's ass and pound him til he shot all his morning load up Josey's ass. Dammm!

They wiped with wet napkins Josey kept in his bag and dressed and left.

"You here every morning?" Josey asked.

"Yes and ready to serve you! As he handed Josey his card.

"I will be back for more!" Josey told him.

"I will be expecting you!" He responded.

Josey got his case and left and was thinking this is a good time to let Rahoul feast for his hole was full!

He had his business for the day completed or did he?

The two studs this morning had made him hotter than normal and now his ass and cock had their own plans.

He checked his Uber to see if Rahoul was nearby and he was!

He ordered a ride and waited for Rahoul to drive up. Ten minutes later he did and Josey could see Rahoul was thinking the same as he did.

Rahoul's pants were already pulled down and a massive size monster dick was laying on the steering wheel rock hard.

Josey wasted no time getting in the front as Rahoul searched for a quiet spot. Josey immediately devoured him right there going half way down the shaft to sloppy wet fuck the huge dick properly.

With Josey bent forward sucking Rahoul's fingers searched for his hairy asshole and loving to finger asses he kept his fingers well filed.
It wasn't long before he was three fingers deep pounding and stretching the ass before him. He let his driver's seat back as Josey climbed on top to ride it deep. There was no pain, just greedy hot pleasure for both of them, ramming and pounding each other with no mercy. Josey laid his face on Rahul's huge muscular hairy chest and licked his nipples as he was rocked with cock.

He felt the first blast as Rahoul blew a load deep in his ass to mix with the previous fuck the saleman's cum.

They rested as the greed slowed down by a tap on the driver's window from a cop in uniform.

It was a quiet out of the way spot so the officer placed a finger to his mouth to order them to be quiet as he opened the door.

He stepped closer into the driver's seat area and told them both.

"Suck me now!" As he pulled out a fat ten inch uncut cock and with no hesitation pushed it in Josey's mouth and throat. He reached down to finger the dick and cum filled ass as Josey performed his best cock worshipper skills on the officer and feeling the head of the dick begin to spray his load coating Josey's throat with the officer's cum.

Gay or bisexual sex is always quick and spontaneous!

When the moment arrives you have to make quick decisions and give your all or take all you want.

Josey licked the dick clean and the officer put it back in his pants as Rahoul kissed Josey to swap the load for he too loved dick sucking and cum.

Josey pulled his pants up and walked to the back of the car and got in. He pulls his pants down exposing his ass as Rahoul feasts on the asshole and loads inside for his morning breakfast.

His ass eating skills were unbelievable and his dick did renovations in Josey's ass he hit the third hole which was much deeper than most ever got too.

That's husband qualifications or atleast a priority friend with benefits.

So much was going on in this one day Josey was overrun with sexual excitement and hunger which seemed to be spreading in the atmosphere around him to others which was a good thing.

It's been said that when your windows of blessings are open extend your arms and open your hands out to be ready to receive and Josey was doing just that!

Rahoul needed to get back to work for this was his job driving people around so he dropped Josey off at work.

Josey sat in his office taking in the morning fun and he was turned on once again so he locked his door and pulled out his throbbing hard cock to stroke out his built up load in his balls. His mind wandered back to each moment and the huge cocks he had devoured and it didn't take long as he spurted a huge continuous load on his desk on a piece of paper covering it with thick white goo!

He didn't hesitate to lick his own load up which was such a mouthful of flavor as the others he had earlier.

He worked hard after that release.

Getting things done was easy today after getting fucked so good and his ass ate by a well skilled tongue.

The ART of eating ass was definitely a skill most did not have like Rahoul does. He planned to get lots more time riding his tongue in the future.

He had a fwb he used to visit on Sundays and ride his tongue in his rim chair for hours with no complaint of his ass situation clean or a lil dirty his bud was going deep with a long tongue. His hairy body kept Josey turned on to stroke and ride his greedy face as he watched porn and others fucking and sucking like them.
There were LIVE Zoom rooms where other guys jacked and sucked and fucked on cam as he rode his fwb with a camera right at the asshole and his face so all could see and one on their hard cocks from above.

Josey loved his fwb pounding his ass with a huge girthy thick cock and loading him with his cum then Josy dump his loads in his throat in the rim chair as he sucked Josey's ass til it was clean of his cum.

Josey rewarded his fwb by pounding his ass in return as well and fisting him deep. Back and forth from dick to fist in the fwb's greedy asshole.This was a regular thing they did weekly keeping each other satisfied and lots of 69 oral plays as porn played in the background.

Sex was Josey's relese mechanism that he used often to keep stress away but sometimes the search for the quality partner brought the stress back. So he learned not to compare or judge his lovers; each was his own entity.

It was late in the day now and Josey had not had lunch just the dicks and cum! He laughed.

A juicy ribeyes with lots of marble fat and rice and gravy with broccoli and mac and cheese and cornbread was now on his mind.

If not a quick stop at a sushi bar spicy eel and salmon and tuna rolls would be quick filling and perfect with noodles.

He was longing for a drive down south to his old southern stomping grounds and have breakfast and brunch at The

Thunderbird off I-95 in Florence, South Carolina or ALL YOU CAN EAT SEAFOOD in Myrtle Beach, South Carolina.

He and his crew Barbara and Dana and L.B. used to burn the bar down there at the beach and walk on the beach and have a cigarette or wine watching the sun come up. Then into the nearest breakfast restaurant to have a fill up on coffee and food!

Dana was BLAH! BLAH! BLAH! Always something to pop off in his mind or out his mouth usually very nasty of course always sex and more sex and his last piece.

L.B. was innocent and THE TRUTH just waiting to call you out!

"DON'T TRY ME BITCHES!" L.B. always insisted.

Barbara was fun and reasoned and very supportive of the big sister of the group. She had the loves of her life but was quick to tolerate their bull for a little while then she would let them go. Only like two since they all knew her. She was definitely NOT THE LOOSE WOMAN! She was A LADY!

L.B. would not let anyone in her private world!
"Always the VIRGIN!" L.B. claimed.

"BULL SHIT!" Dana knew a few of his accomplished hits but pretended to be right along with him.

WASHINGTON, D.C. was ALL THE WAY LIVE 24/7 and the gay bars packed up early for drinks and MEN!

A vodka and juice or brandy and cola was always an instant with a shot of tequila.

Weed is GOOD TOO! In moderation.

These guys ruining their lives on meth or excuse me CLOUDS was JUST FUKN CRAZY!

NO MATTER WHAT IT IS YOU SHOULD NOT DO IT ALL DAM DAY EVERYDAY!

Even though a big dick or bubble ass CAN BE VERY TEMPTING!
Josey thought.

  The guys in the bar called The Fireplace in D.C. near a gay cruising park was HOT AND TEMPTING!

You could drink up enough courage or get stupid enough to walk in the park and fuck or suck cocks!
It was there if you chose to go to the DRAG BARS and watch sissies GIVING YOU FEM LIFE OUT LOUD!

The funny thing about guys that dress in dresses and perform is that MOST OF THEM ARE TOPS!

They pursue a good ass way more than a big dick that is just something EXTRA!

After meeting up with friends and

YADDY, YADDY,YADDY, YADDY!

Which is what Josey and Dana called chatting!

 Gay men talking just diarrhea of the mouth saying Anything and Everything OUT LOUD!

YES! YOU MIGHT GET YOUR TOES STEPPED ON!

SO WATCH IT WHEN YOU WEARING YOUR BEST PUMPS OUT IN PUBLIC!
BECAUSE A BITCH NEAR YOU MIGHT BE SPILLING YOUR TEA!
TO EVERY AND ANYBODY IN THE BAR AND ON SOCIAL MEDIA AS WELL!

BE VICIOUS!

As Dana and L.B. would CHEER!

"GET HER! GET THAT BITCH! GET HER! GET HER!"

Both laughing and high fives and CACKLING!

Some Gays will cross grey lines into unchartered territories and then...

"THEIR ASS IS GRASS!"

" READY TO BE MOWED!"

"YOU CAN'T JUST WALK ON SOMEONE JUST BECAUSE YOU WANT TOO!"
"YOU BETTER BRING SOME EXTRA LEGS!"

L.B. Always said.

"CAUSE SISSIES WILL CUT YOU
OFF AT THE KNEES WORSE
THAN DIABETES!" He added.

"L.B. When are you going to get you a
husband?"
Barbara asked him.

"Yes! Whore ain't it time for you to
SETTLE DOWN?"
Josey said laughing.

"YES! Give your COOCHIE AND
YOUR JAWS A BREAK BITCH!"
Dana said.

"I AM NOT YOU BITCHES FOOL!"

"I see yall asses hurt and struggling and stds! NO THANK YOU HOES!" L.B. replied.

"Yall asses needed to wake the fuck up!"
He said.

"Ain't NOTHING IN THESE STREETS BUT HOES!"
L.B. told them.

"HOES RAISING MORE HOES!"

"Keep the family legends going!" He laughed.

"FUCKEM ALL BITCHES!"
Dana said laughing.

"AND THE GOOD ONES TWICE!"
L.B. added.

"FWB!" Josey told them.

"HELL YES!" They all said.

"When are we all going to Nawleans or Vegas?"
Dana asked.

"As Soon as we are sure you are not on the same BITCHY ASS MEDS YOU WAS ON IN NEW YORK!"

"YOU WAS A CRAZY ASS HEFFA BITCH!"
Josey told him.

"YES! I was on generic SHIT!"

"THAT GABAPATIN will FUCK YOUR MIND UP!"
Dana told them.

"My dematologist told me throw that SHIT IN THE TRASH before I commit suicide!" He added.

"OH! REALLY!" Barbara asked.

"GURRL WHICH TRASH CAN DID YOU THROW IT IN? DO YOU REMEMBER?" Josey asked.

"OH HELL NAW YOU DIDN'T!"
L.B. responded.

"Sissies would have sold that shit fifty
dollars a pill!"
Josey said laughing.

"DAMMM!"

"I didn't think about that!" Dana
laughed.

"NO I DON'T DO ILLEGAL SHIT!"
He added.

"Sucking dick in a public park at night
IS ILLEGAL BITCH! YOU DO
THAT!"

L.B. told him.

"GURRL I WOULD NEVER DO THAT!"
Dana replied.

"BITCH PLEASE!"
BARBARA, JOSEY AND L.B. SAID IN REPLY OUT LOUD!

"YALL JUST JEALOUS!"
Dana answered.

"SMELL HIS BREATH!"
L.B. said.

"EWWWW!"
Josey replied.

"YOU KNOW IT SMELLS A CUMMY MESS OF ASS AND DICKS!"
Josey said laughing while checking his own.

"DID YOU SEE THIS BITCH CHECKING HIS OWN BREATH ON THE SLY?"
L.B. said laughing.

"SHIT! WAIT A MINUTE!" L.B. Said checking his own.

"DON'T YOU TRY MS. TUNA HELPER AND STARKIST TUNA OVER HERE MS. BARBARA!"
Dana said to her pointing.

"OH! HELL NAW!" She replied.

"YEAH! SHE PROBABLY BUMBLE BEE OR WALMART GREAT VALUE SIX PACK!"
L.B. Said screaming!

"FUCK ALL YALL ON A CRUISE FOR US!"
Dana told them.

"GREG IS GOING TOO! AND KEERON TOO!
YOU KNOW BOTH ARE FUN!"

"AND WE WILL HAVE A THREE BEDROOM SUITE WITH BALCONY AND BUTLER!"

"BARBARA YOU BRINGING YOUR LADY?

"We got to book this SOON!"

"HELL YEAH!" They agree.

"AND IT STAYS 24 HOURS IN NEW ORLEANS PORT BEFORE WE GO TO THE DOMINICAN REPUBLIC AND BAHAMAS!"

"OKAY BITCHES AND MUTHER FUCKERS!"

"WE GOING!"

"ITS ON!" Dana shouts!